Stupid

Kyuka Lilymjok

ISBN 978-978-974-150-2

Published by:
Free Pen Publishers
10 Lachlan Close, Maitama, Abuja

Any people depicted in stock imagery provided by Thinkstock are models, and such images are being used for such purposes only.

This book is printed on acid-free paper.

The views expressed in this work are solely those of the author and do not necessarily reflect the views of the publisher. The publisher hereby disclaims any responsibility for them.

To my wife Maria and my children: Justice, Sunfair and Fairprincess

Though the cup
is empty, it is full
in the eyes of
the fool

Chapter One

I had a fortunate or an unfortunate start in life depending on which way one views or understands my circumstances. I was born by rich parents in the dying years of the African slave trade. My father was a slave merchant and I grew up to inherit his trade.

As a slave merchant, my father initially used to take slaves to the white slave traders along the West African Coast. As a child, I used to accompany him to the coast whenever he was taking slaves to sell to white men slave buyers at the coast. The first time I accompanied him, I can still remember his gleeful face when he delivered three slaves to the white men and was given a mirror, tobacco, pieces of cloths and rum. Smiling into the mirror, he was full of mirth and satisfaction. His happiness and satisfaction seemed to grow when he drank the rum. When he drank the rum, his head rolled on his neck as he beamed with joy into the mirror. I stood beside him also enchanted by the mirror. What magical instrument was this that reproduces one's face? I kept wondering and even my father in his drunken state kept wondering like me.

When my father became a more established slave merchant, the white men slave traders sometimes used to come to buy slaves from him at his little fort along the Bwabwa River. I was always at the fort with him when he sold slaves to the white men. Most of the slaves he sold were people he raided in their farms while they were farming or harvesting their crops. Others were travelers moving through the forest. He raided people for his slave trade using three hefty men he employed for the task who he paid nickels for their sweat. Even as a child, I used to wonder how these men called shantas would undertake such a dangerous and cruel task for such payments.

My father raided people for his slave trade mostly by kidnapping them. The three hefty men kidnapped people by sneaking on them and overpowering them with brute force or a dragnet before chaining them and handing them over to my father. Chained and helpless, they were a pathetic sight. Before being sold to the white men they were kept in a shack or under the scourging sun and poorly fed. If they were to be taken to the coast to be sold, they trekked all the way to the coast and with whips on their backs on any misdemeanour or even misstep. In chains and knowing the fate that awaits them, the anguish on their faces sometimes pricked my heart.

If his men found no one to kidnap, my father bought slaves from African slave owners and resold them to the white men. Because he was rarely in want of slaves to sell to the white men, the white men considered him one of their very important slave merchants.

When I was twenty, an incident that was to haunt me for most of my life happened. A rebellious slave that refused to move as the slaves were being walked to the coast for sale to the white men was flogged with a thong to death. Not far from our house, the slave a strong young man about my age dug his feet into the ground and refused to move. He was flogged, kicked and pushed but he would not move. All the while he refused to move, he kept saying he would rather die than be sold into slavery. While flogging him with the thong that ate into his flesh, I could see both my father and the man flogging him wincing whenever the whip landed on his bare back. This told me they were not enjoying what they were doing. Why then were they doing it? It was much later I knew they were propelled by the greed for gain to do what they did.

On my part, my heart was torn whenever the thong landed on the back of the man. While the thong was tearing his back, it was tearing my heart. Despite my feelings then however, I grew up to inherit my father's trade instead of despising it, and to be as mean and cruel as he was.

After a long time of being flogged, the man folded up on his legs and stretched out on the ground. The shanta kicked him to stand up, but only his lifeless body rolled over. He was dead. Both the shanta and my father exchanged fleeting glances of terror and guilt.

'Is he dead?' my father asked the shanta.

'It seems so,' the shanta said bending to shake the lifeless body on the ground.

'Oh my God,' my father mourned.

Hearing him say 'Oh my God,' I wondered if my father had God; if he had one, if his God was not angry with him. I also wondered if he was mourning out of guilt or for the loss of what the dead slave would have fetched him.

'You shouldn't have killed him,' my father whined

'We shouldn't have killed him,' the Shanta corrected him. 'I was acting on your instruction.'

For days and years, the image of this man writhing on the ground in pain as he was being pelted with the thong tormented me. I later discovered my father did not fare much better than me. He had nightmares and sometimes woke up in the night screaming.

Chapter Two

From childhood, I had always been obsessed with wealth and having things others did not have. I wanted to wear clothes others could not afford and shoes others could not. Colourful and glamorous things excited me to no end while drab things repulsed me to distraction. Whenever I came by poor and pitiable circumstances, nausea rises from the pit of my stomach to my mouth, revulsion and contempt were visibly branded on my face like the shadow of Auyu.* My love for the good things of life pushed my quest for wealth into overdrive so that I could afford these things. Waxing literal, in my overdrive for wealth, pedestrians – poor people, were meat to my tyres.

I not only craved for the good things of the earth, I craved for the good things of the hereafter. I wanted to make it in heaven the way I thought I was making it on earth. Three happenings early in my life should have tempered the rigor of my obsession with wealth and material things, but alas I did not heed any

---

* The shadow of Auyu was a dense shadow a ghost was said to have left permanently in Auyu.

of these happenings. I carried on as if nothing had happened.

First, my father died from a very painful, protracted sickness that reduced him to a mere skeleton. Both the drum and the flute were going quiet for him and there was no bird to dance for him. There was neither wind nor sail that could serve him. He was beyond hail and past signal. His ship was sunk and he was only with a white flag to wave at the grim reaper.

Few days to his death, he could not eat because there were sores in his mouth and throat that made eating impossible. Whenever he made an effort to eat, tears fell from his eyes from the pain of trying to eat. As eating was painful to him, lying down on the bed was also painful because there were also sores on his body. He kept turning on his bed without finding a comfortable part of his body to lie on. He could neither sit nor stand up because he was too weak for any of these. Two days to his death, my father was begging and pleading for death, but death refused to come.

Whenever I looked at my father on his sickbed and remembered who and what he was when he was well, I wept disconsolately. My father was richer than everyone in our town, but the poorest person in the town was now better than him. He could afford any horse, but was now incapable of riding any horse. It was poor people who could not afford donkeys that were capable of riding horses. He could afford any food and any dress, but now was incapable of eating any food and wearing any dress. It was poor people who could not afford any of these things that were now capable of enjoying them. The irony was searing and dementing.

How and why did this strange sickness that defies cure come into my father's body? What bad things had he done to deserve the punishment of this painful and protracted sickness? Even as I asked these questions, I knew a number of bad things my father had done particularly to his slaves that merited nemesis. Many slaves had died in his hands on the way to the coast under torturous conditions. Many had died from fatigue and hunger brought upon them by him. All of them had been rudely separated from their families and were never seen again by those they loved and those that loved them. Their heartaches, the heartaches of their relations were immeasurable.

Were the ill-treated slaves my father captured and sold to the white men hitting back? If they were, they were more heartless than my father. Nothing he did to them deserved this kind of punishment. Yes, my father did bad capturing and selling them into slavery. But he was only trying to get by in a world everyone is struggling to get by. Why should they take it out on him in such a cruel and heartless manner? He was not the one who started slavery. He met it in the world and only tried to get by on it.

The second happening that should have made me realize the folly of my obsession with wealth, colour and glamour was when a woman I knew in her prime to be very beautiful and glamorous like my father became afflicted by a strange sickness. In no time, all her beauty withered away. Those that used to admire her now flinched whenever they saw her. Before she died taking her erstwhile beauty and glamour into the grave, she was avoided by everyone and was a very unhappy person.

The third happening that should have reordered my life was the reverse in the fortunes of a white man slave merchant my father used to sell slaves to. This slave merchant used to be the richest white man my father sold slaves to. He dressed better than all the other white men and bought slaves at better prices. Later I was no longer seeing him at the coast where we used to take slaves to him and I inquired after him. I was told he had fallen on evil days and no longer had money to buy slaves. I was told he had lost his money in an investment that failed and was now going to the wall for bread.

I should have learned bitter lessons of life from these happenings, but I seemed a man incapable of repenting of my folly, a man doomed to run his life on error. So I carried on with my life heedless of good lessons life was passing to me; never forgetting to be stupid and never missing any opportunity to be stupid. Wisdom was coming to me from different sources, but it was like air balloons thrown at a porcupine.

Chapter Three

I got to know the oppression and injustice the slaves suffered in the hands of my father and his shantas was nothing compared to what they suffered at sea with the white men they were sold to and what they suffered in the plantations they eventually worked. From their behaviour on the coast, the white men did not seem to consider the Africans who sold slaves to them or the slaves sold to them human. While they put up a show of considering Africans that sold slaves to them as human, now and then the façade on their faces slipped and the contempt they had for those selling slaves to them showed. As for the slaves, they put up no pretence on how they see them: they were merchandise they had bought from which they expected the highest returns.

At sea on their way to Europe, the slaves were chained to each other and arranged in rows where they ate and defecated; where they were flogged and kicked for perceived misbehaviour; where they cried and died. Those who died on board the ship, their corpses were thrown into the sea. Those who survived the horrors of the trip to Europe were delivered by the ship to another phase of agony. From the sea in Europe they trekked to the destination of their owners or were carried in horses or oxen drawn wagons to the destination depending on its distance from the sea. The destination was usually the farm or plantation they would work.

By the farm or plantation, the slaves were quartered in sleazy makeshift barracks or hostels with no room to swing a cat. Most of these barracks and hostels were constructed with wood and logs. Virtually all slaves lived where they worked – kitchens, laundries and stables. The economic calculation was clear: Slave owners did not want the additional cost of moving slaves from their residential quarters to where they work. Work-time lost in moving slaves from accommodations not on work-sites was another consideration. Living where they worked, slaves worked all day through and even at night when there was the need of doing so.

On the farms and plantations, the slaves worked with little rest and little food. If out of fatigue they lagged or fell behind in their work, they were flogged by the taskmaster whose whip was never far from their hides. Most farms and plantations that slaves worked on were farms and plantations of cotton, rice, corn, sugarcane and tobacco. The slaves did the backbreaking labour of tilling the land, planting the crops, weeding and harvesting them. Hundreds of slaves worked in big plantations the year round. Rice plantations in most cases were the most deadly. Slaves stood inside water for hours working under blistering heat. If there was less work in their farms or plantation, slaves were hired out for days or even for years all in a bid for the master to maximize his profit from the slave.

Drivers, overseers and masters were responsible for farm and plantation discipline which they enforced ruthlessly against erring slaves. There was a slave code that spelt out what a slave must not do. For instance, a slave could not leave his plantation or farm without permission, strike a white man even in self-defence, gather without white presence or visit the home of a white man. Drivers, overseers and masters enforced slave code sparing no indulgence for any slave. The killing of a slave was not considered murder and raping a black woman was treated as mere trespass.

Slaves cleared land for cultivation, dug ditches, cut and haul wood, slaughtered livestock, made repairs to buildings and tools. They also worked as blacksmiths, drivers, and carpenters. Some slaves worked as domestics providing services for the overseer's or master's family. These were house servants different from field slaves. The lot of house servants on the surface might look better than that of field slaves, in reality however, this is often not the case. House servants were constantly under the scrutiny of their masters and mistresses, could be called for work anytime and had no privacy.

Slaves were badly fed and were forced to work even when they were sick. They lived under the constant fear of being sold in an auction if their master is hard-up for cash or if he wanted to punish them for a real or perceived misdeed. If this happened, parents might be separated from their children by the parents or children being sold to another master.

Though white slave masters did not consider black people human beings, they slept with black women consensually or by rape. Seeing black people as animals but sleeping with black women, they were involved in some form of bestiality. If they raped the women, they were bestial in a double sense. Sexual intercourse between white men and black women in most cases led to pregnancy and the birth of mulattos thereby making the case that black people were human like white people.

Much later, I learned slaves were driven to produce crops than slave owners could handle. I also learned some slave owners were tired of their slaves and wanted to sell them, but did not get buyers. Some of these slave owners wanted their slaves to leave, but the slaves refused to leave. I also heard of cases slaves were driven to revolt by overbearing drivers, overseers and masters. When I heard of all these things, I wondered the intelligence and wisdom of those who bought slaves and drove them to revolt by hardship.

Chapter Four

On one of my trips to the coast with my father to deliver slaves to the white men, the slaves we brought were thrown into a sleazy, stinking ship whose odour made me vomit though I had not entered it. The ship was a hole that had been degraded to a pigsty. Standing a little far off the sea, I could hear my father and another slave dealer who had brought slaves to the white men talking about the filthy condition of the ship the slaves were thrown into.

'That ship has not had a bath for a long time,' I heard the other slave merchant whose name I later knew to be Oyoto saying to my father.

'One would have thought a ship inside water has no need for bathing, but this is proving not the case,' my father said. 'Water carries its own dirt that requires water to wash it.'

'You are saying something there,' Oyoto said.

'Though the fish is inside water, it also takes its bath like all of us,' my father said.

'I wonder how a white man can stand the kind of stench issuing out of this ship,' Oyoto said. 'It turns my intestines round.'

'The stench does not get to them,' my father said. 'They are in the cabin of the ship that is insulated from the stench of the hull.'

'I sometimes wonder if there is something to crow about this trade,' Oyoto said, sighing expansively.

'The cock crows not necessarily because there is something to crow about,' my father said in a rare access to intelligence.

'I am not a cock,' Oyoto said without a rise in his humour.'

'Neither am I,' my father said.

'I sometimes wonder if what I am getting from this trade is anything close to the suffering the slaves I sell to the white men go through,' Oyoto pressed on in an impassioned tone. 'These slaves can equally work for me instead of selling them to the white men who they work for making them rich. When exchanging these slaves for rum, mirrors and tobacco, I sometimes feel like I am exchanging millet for chaff or a cow for milk.'

'You call mirrors, tobacco and rum chaff?' my father asked with a look of surprise on his face. 'Without mirrors you will die without knowing what you look like. 'Everyone will know you, but you will not know yourself.'

'I was doing well knowing what I look like by the waters of our streams and rivers before the mirrors came,' Oyoto said. 'Beside I am not a handsome person; why should I be staring into mirrors for what does not fascinate me?'

Oyoto was by far more handsome than my father. Why was he saying he was not a handsome man? Was he mocking my father? I looked at my father to see if he was thinking the way I was thinking but found he was not. The smug expression he always carried was still branded on his face. I shrugged my shoulders. 'What of the rum and tobacco that makes your head roll on your neck giving you a glimpse of the hereafter?' I heard my father asking Oyoto again. 'Are these things also chaff?'

'I was doing well by gyand which sends me to sleep with a smile before the coming of rum and tobacco,' Oyoto said.

'What of the clothes? Are they also chaff? If they are, where are your grains?' my father asked.

'I was doing well with the woolen toga before the coming of the white man's clothes,' Oyoto said. 'Honestly, Kunse we are losing more in this nefarious trade than we are gaining.'

'I don't know about that,' my father said. Though he said this, I could see a slight look of uncertainty creeping into his eyes.

'I know about that,' Oyoto said. 'What these slaves go through here is nothing compared to what they go through at sea and in the white man's land if they survived the sea and make it to the white man's land. Crammed together in the ship like spoons, they are tossed against the ship and each other at sea bruising themselves. In the white man's land, they are taken to plantations where they work more than cows and donkeys.'

'Well, that is what slavery is all about,' my father said. 'From the beginning of time, slaves have always worked more than cows and donkeys.'

'There is nothing to crow about this trade,' Oyoto said more to himself than to my father.

'I won't exactly say so,' my father said.

'Because of what I know of this trade, I am seriously thinking of quitting the trade,' Oyoto said in a dramatic tone.

'You can't be serious,' my father said with a mild look of alarm.

'Unfortunately, I am,' Oyoto said. 'If we were making great fortunes in the trade, the fortunes would make up for the curses of the trade. But we are not making fortunes. We are only attracting curses. It is not wise continuing the trade, at least on its current terms.'

'Hmm ...,' my father snorted

'We are making sense sad,' Oyoto said.

My father did not say anything. He did not even appear to have heard what Oyoto said. If he heard him, he did not seem to grasp the import of what he said.

'Wisdom is laughing at us,' Oyoto said.

'What are you saying?' my father asked looking puzzled.

'Intelligence is embarrassed by us,' Oyoto continued his cynical remarks.

'Hmm ...,' my father hummed looking vacuous.

'Intelligence is ashamed of us,' Oyoto said again.

Again, my father did not say anything. He only stood looking at Oyoto with an expression on his face that told me this time he understood what Oyoto said and seemed to be saying in his mind if intelligence was ashamed of them, it may as well go and hang itself.

After this conversation, I did not see Oyoto again in any of my trips to the coast with my father to deliver slaves to the white men. But I could not say whether I was not seeing him because he had quit the trade or because we were at the coast on different days. Not knowing which was the case, I asked my father.

'Honestly, I don't know,' my father said. 'But given the way he spoke about the trade the last time we were together, I won't be surprised if he had quitted.'

Though I wanted to ask my father if like Oyoto he was thinking of giving up the trade, I could not summon the courage to do so. It was against the tradition of respect for a father I had been brought up by.

Chapter Five

My father did not leave his slave trade business till his death. When he died, I inherited the assets and liabilities of his trade. Like Oyoto, Initially I had misgivings about the trade and once in a while suffered remorse for the suffering of the slaves. What I say here about myself is a summary of my character. Now and then I knew the right thing to do and even had the conscience to do it; but driven by excessive love for gain and wealth, I will not do the right thing and would have little or no remorse for doing the wrong thing.

To return to my misgivings on slave trade, my misgivings soon disappeared and any conscience I had against the trade with it. Instead of being ashamed of the trade, I was arrogant and prideful over the wealth I acquired from the trade. Unlike during my father's time, during my time slaves were no longer paid for with mirrors, rum, tobacco and cloths, they were paid for in pound sterling and the franc. There were also more fanciful things now to be purchased with the money the trade yielded.

My arrogance had no temperance on it. Without the leash of temperance, my arrogance carried a whip and odour that announced my presence wherever I went. The whip whizzed and whirred in the air as I swirled it about while the odour oozed and purred out of my carriage and what I said. With arrogance in my legs and mouth, not many people desired my society much.

In addition to being arrogant, I was vain, greedy and over ambitious – dispositions I later found quite unfortunate. While wanting to have all the good things the world could offer, I wanted to also have all the good things there was in the hereafter and I would stop at nothing to have my way in everything I wanted. For a while, I succeeded in having my cravings, but later things started falling apart for me.

Despite my failings, I wanted to have many friends and was always aggrieved I had few. My friendship with people never last. I initially did not know why until much later. Later, I saw myself as a porcupine whose quills of pride and arrogance made no distinction between his friends and foes.

Dimma was the first friend I was very close to. He was a man who always carried a cloudy face wherever he went. Beside me, he had no known friend. People do not always want to be beaten by rain. With clouds on his face, it was said people kept away from him not knowing when the clouds on his face would turn to rain and fall on them. But I made a friend of him perhaps believing I always dressed in colourful attire was a rainbow of sort that in the traditional belief of my village will always prevent rain from falling, no matter the clouds.

Like me, Dimma was also a trader. Unlike me however, Dimma traded in cocoa, not slaves. Unlike me still, Dimma was a very humble and stoic person fortune or the lack of it had little or no visible influence on. For the most part, he seemed to me a man who lived outside circumstances and so was unaffected by them. Prices of cocoa would rise; there would be no excitement in Dimma. Prices of cocoa would fail; there would be no depression in Dimma. He had money; you won't know. He did not have money; you won't also know.

Every time I was at sea to deliver slaves to the white man, I was always excited by the rising and falling waves of the sea. A wave built up from the sea and increased in volume and height as it neared the coast; then it would fall and rolled back in undertows as it reached the coast. When the wave was building and rising, I was in it with excitement. When it fell, I was in it with depression. Later, I came to see rising and falling prices of slaves as the rising and falling of sea waves. When prices of slaves rose, I was in the wave of the rising prices with excitement, and when they fell, I was in the fall with depression.

Unlike me, Dimma in the cocoa trade was never in the waves of rising or falling cocoa prices. Not excited by a rise in cocoa price, he could not be depressed by a fall in prices of the commodity.

'Dimma, I am surprised you are not excited by the boom in cocoa prices,' I said to my friend when cocoa prices rose steeply.

'If cocoa prices are rising, cocoa prices will fall,' Dimma said in his usual temperate tone. 'Whatever rises, falls because the sky is not a place things perch on for long. I try not to expect much in life; not expecting much, I am not disappointed much.'

'You are lucky Dimma to be outside feelings,' I said in a voice clouded with emotions. 'Booming prices do not boom you; and depressing prices do not depress you. How are you able to rise above circumstances without any wave?'

'I am able to do so because I don't see much in life,' Dimma said drily.

'Why don't you see much in life?'

'Because there is actually not much in life.'

'Hmm ...'

'While struggling to be something, I know that in the end, I can only be nothing; while struggling to earn a living, I know that in the end I can only earn death. The facts and terms of life are nasty. From a very early time, I, albeit grudgingly, accepted to live with the rude facts of life the way I found them,' Dimma pontificated with sour philosophical calmness.

Was what he just said the clouds in his eyes? I wondered. Most likely I thought. Has the futility he saw in life turned to a brooding and resentful cloud on his face? Most likely I thought.

Dimma ought to have been a mirror I would view not only life but myself; but alas he was not. I carried on with him the same arrogant and self-conceited way I had always carried on with everyone unfortunate to relate with me. Somehow Dimma endured me for a long time may be because of who he was. But we eventually broke off because I tried his patience beyond tolerance limits.

I had high taste for clothes and dressed very well. Dressing fashionably, I was seen by many as a dandy. One of the reasons, I treasured the trade on slaves with the white men was the access it gave me to good clothes they bought the slaves with if they were short of cash. Consciously and unconsciously, I always had a haughty, condescending attitude to anyone shabbily dressed.

Unlike me, Dimma did not care about his appearance. Perhaps thinking the clouds on his face would turn to rain and drench his clothes, he dressed only to cover his nakedness and nothing more. He was not only always poorly dressed, he sometimes appeared to me to have contempt for well-dressed people like me – an attitude I thought strange. If any trace of arrogance was to be found in him, I felt it would be in his attitude to those better dressed than him. It was bad enough that he was threadbare. Why show contempt for those well-clad? Must we all wear rags? If we wear all the rags in the world, what would the mad men wear?

Dimma's attitude to dressing was something I resented in him and turned out to be what ended our friendship. When we broke off because of our different attitudes to dressing, I was rather surprised we did not break off much earlier on account of this difference. We were attending a marriage ceremony and I turned up as usual in my classy clothes while Dimma as usual turned up in his tasteless attire. So bad was his dressing that he appeared to me this day worse than I had ever seen him. The clothes he wore looked like he borrowed them from the mad man I used to see near the market square at Dikwa. Indeed, when I first saw him, I thought it was this mad man I was seeing. Going to the wedding ceremony with him, I had a haunting sense of wearing his rags with him and this gave me a creepy feeling.

Apart from dressing so badly for this event, Dimma had this haughty look in his face that not only suggested pride in his appearance, but contempt for those differently dressed. This touched off my anger. Since when had it become the place of trashy men to look down on those adorned in royal robes instead of the other way round? 'Why are you dressed in sack clothes like Job, and to a wedding, not a funeral ceremony?' I asked in a very contemptuous voice. 'Why are you always appearing as if you wear your clothes with pigs? Dimma, you disgust me the way a pig from the village muddy pond does.'

'And you Tata disgust me the way gaudiness disgust me,' Dimma said in the snootiest manner I had ever heard him speak. The clouds on his face had turned to rain and the rain was falling on me.

'What!' I exclaimed in shock.

'Because the dog was patted on the back by a princess, it began thinking it is a prince who might one day marry the princess,' Dimma said, contempt leaping out of his eyes to drench me. The rain had turned to hail and blizzard and I was without cover.

'Well, Dimma I can't be suffered to wear your rags with you wshile I am wearing my kingly garments,' I said with equal contempt. 'I cannot because I am the friend of a swine wear mud for clothes,' I went on with an imperial air.

'If you insist on being a sow, you may go your swinish way while I go my peacock way.'

'So be it,' Dimma said and walked away from me as I was also walking away from him. It turned out we were not only walking away from each other but also from our friendship. Since that day, Dimma and I ceased to be friends.

Chapter Six

Those who knew me and Dimma as friends used to refer to us as the pig and the peacock – Dimma the pig and I the Peacock. The pig is unsightly in appearance while the peacock was comely. This characterization was mostly by those who knew us only by appearance. Those who knew us beyond appearance knew Dimma was the peacock and I was the pig. He was in the seemly and becoming trade of buying and selling cocoa; I was in the unseemly and unbecoming trade of raiding, buying and selling slaves. He was humble; I was arrogant. No doubt I carried beautiful feathers. But below those feathers were the mud of a pig.

Sometimes when I paused to ponder my obsession with regal dressing, I wondered if I was trying to launder myself of the dirt of my trade and manners by dressing exquisitely; I wondered if my dressing was perfume worn by a man who had gone for weeks without bathing. I wondered if under the illusion of my dressing, I was dancing naked in the village square while Dimma poorly dressed was the one dancing well-dressed in the village square.

There was a river I repaired to for solitude. Sitting by the river one day, I saw a beautiful butterfly flitting about. I was so enchanted by this butterfly that my eyes followed it wherever it went. Perching on a blade of grass not far from where I was, a lizard pounced on the butterfly. The beautiful butterfly folded into the mouth of the lizard and was seen no more. I was angry; I was sad; I felt trashed. Why is it that it is the ugly and contemptible things of life that destroy the beautiful and enchanting things of life? Why is life always favouring ugly things against beautiful ones? With all its beauty, the butterfly was nothing more than food for a lizard. I felt pursued. I felt betrayed. I felt rubbished.

That butterfly! So beautiful; so royal. Was it flaunting beauty or royalty before it was devoured by the contemptible reptile? Whatever it was flaunting, it had been reduced to dung by a nauseating thing. It seemed apart from me nothing is bothered by the death of the butterfly. The grasses were swaying as they had always swayed and the water in the river was flowing as it had always flowed. The birds were flying in the sky as they had always flown and perching on trees as they had always perched.

While sitting by the river, a fisherman moving downstream with his hook, line and sinker fishing came by where I was sitting looking like I had been stung by a wasp. The fisherman knew me and I knew him. We exchanged greetings.

'Tata why are you looking like the world has crumbled about you?' the fisherman asked me.

'The world has not really crumbled on me Tuche, but it had just crumbled on a butterfly I loved,' I said.

'A butterfly?'

'Yes, a butterfly.'

'Tata, where did you meet the butterfly and fell in love with it?' Tuche asked me with an amused expression on his face.

'By the bank of this river,' I said in a forlorn tone. It seemed talking about the butterfly with Tuche was making me sadder.

'What happened to the butterfly?'

'It was eaten up by a lizard.'

'It was lucky it was not eaten up by a bush rat. Bush rats are more vicious than lizards.'

I did not say anything. I was wondering if it mattered to the butterfly that was eaten what ate it.

'Tata, I have always suspected you of madness,' Tuche said in a derisive voice. 'What you are saying now is removing any doubt I had on the matter before.' Saying this, he moved downstream with his line, hook and sinker.

Tuche was moving on the bank of the river holding the stick on which the line was tied. The sinker was somewhere in the middle of the line while the hook carrying the bait was at the tail end of the line. The hook and the bait were always inside the water waiting for a hungry and indiscreet fish while the sinker as always was floating on the water. Now and then the sinker nose-dived to tell the fisherman a fish was nibbling the bait and therefore he was near a catch. When this happened, the fisherman fed more line to the river. From the slight way the sinker sank into the water, it seemed the fish nibbling the bait was a smart fish. It was cleverly eating up the bait leaving the hook. This seemed to irritate the fisherman from the expression on his face. Now and then he pulled out the hook from the water to examine the bait or what remained of it on the hook.

My eyes were riveted on the sinker as it floated on the water and as it occasionally sank into the water on a pull by the fish. After a while, the sinker was no longer diving. It seemed the fish had eaten up the whole bait on the hook and had swam away. Behold when the fisherman pulled the hook out of the water, there was no bait on it. From where I sat, I could hear him cursing and swearing at the fish. He was now looking like another being the world had crumbled on. I smiled to myself. 'Life,' I muttered.

Chapter Seven

In the course of my life as a slave merchant, I not only sold slaves, I owned slaves that worked in my farmlands. These slaves worked fourteen hours a day; often with little food in their stomachs. I only thought of the wealth they were creating for me. If they died doing so, it was the loss of their labour that was of concern to me, not their death. I had a cruel slave taskmaster whose whip ate the backs of the slaves more than their hands eked wealth for me from the soil. This slave taskmaster was so cruel that the slaves dreaded him more than the hard work they were forced to do. Several times I had eavesdropped on the slaves talking about the ill-treatment they received from this taskmaster, but I never rebuked him to refrain from his cruel treatment of the slaves. I felt he was doing the right thing because I have always thought the only way to get slaves to work well for you is to be harsh to them.

'Our taskmaster carries wickedness and cruelty in a sac the way a snake carries poison in a sac,' said one of the slaves to another while they were working and their taskmaster was not within earshot.

'Where the milk of human kindness is in other human beings is where his sac of cruelty is,' said the other slave.

'All his life, he seems bitter about something; what it is I can't place a finger,' said the first slave.

'Maybe he is bitter about the curse placed on him by the creator of all human beings for his wickedness of making man sin against the creator,' said the second slave. 'This man I tell you is the hand of Satan stretched against the world. He is someone chased out of the Garden of Eden.'

'Why can't he and our owner who is not any better understand that to get the best out of us, he should give us the best,' said the first slave. 'Why are they going to cruelty for the good they seek instead of to kindness? Why are they using a basket to fetch water instead of a bucket?'

Because the slaves were overworked and ill-treated, they grew old faster and therefore could not do much work in the farm. As little blood can be bled out of an anaemic patient, old and tired, little labour could be bled out of these slaves. Now and then they revolted against the harsh conditions they lived and worked. When they revolted, the work in the farm suffered and I suffered severe losses.

While my slave taskmaster was handing down raw deals to my slaves in the farm and they were groaning under his tyranny, I was in town in all my colours of pride and arrogance unchecked by the humble beginning and humble end of life. For me, life remained a royal chariot of majesty and a rolling party of fun. Every day I went into town dressed in one of my colourful dresses full of pomp and pageantry. Behind me and in front of me would be servants I barked orders to. Unknown to me as I was barking orders to them life was barking orders at me to come down my high horse.

Within my life time our town had grown from a small town to a fairly big one. There were paved streets with shops here and there mainly selling provisions and petty wares. On whichever street I was, I had many people staring at me, some jeering, while others cheering. Most of the people staring at me were likely people seeing me for the first time. Most of those jeering or cheering were likely those who knew me before.

I was popularly called *the Maghot* – the colourful one. When walking on the road in my garish colours, shouts of 'there goes the Maghot in all the colours of the world!' rent the air. For the most part, when on the street, I was a peacock gliding through the street with his tail spread out. With my tail fanned out and my gait in the air, I walked through the street with the pleasure of a monarch going through his domain hailed by his subjects. However, to many folks, I was a saddle on a sow and a fellow way out of the city gate of seeming appearance and grace.

In the evenings when the sun cast a long shadow on me that was grotesque, I was sometimes angry with the sun for doing a caricature of royalty. Distinction was abroad and the sun should attend mannerly.

On the street, I was a moving train of royalty trampling everything underfoot. I hearken to nothing but expected everything to hearken to me. Wealth had gotten into my head and I had gone bunkers with pride and arrogance. I was beyond whistle and beyond advice. My sober uncle who was whistling to me seeking to give me wise counsel, I hearkened not to, but plunged on into life like a wanton horse that lost his rein in a stampede. Though I never hearken to any of my uncle's wise counsel, I never forgot one occasion he spoke to me so solemnly.

'Tata,' my uncle on this occasion said to me in a cautionary tone when I had done an unseemly thing.

'Uncle,' I intoned.

'If the wind is telling you stupid things, why are you not telling the wind what you are seeing and hearing from life is different from what it is telling you? If it is telling you nonsense, why are you not telling yourself the sense you are seeing and hearing from life?'

I said nothing. I only gawped at him.

'Tata,' my uncle called me a second time; 'the wind is carrying you on its wings and will drop you where you can't pick your pieces,' he said with his piercing eyes lancing me. 'Before you, it carried your father; where did it drop him?'

Again, I said nothing as I continued to gawp at him.

'I know you are saying in your mind you would rather enjoy the flight in the wind than trek all the days of your life to your grave,' he went on more in a resigned tone than a hopeful one. 'Before you, your father said the same thing; but could not say the same thing when the wind dropped him where it dropped him. Not only did the wind drop him on a hard place, it laughed at him when it dropped him. Standing here talking to you his impetuous son hard of hearing, I can still hear the wind laughing at him where it dropped him.'

For the third time, I said nothing.

'Tata,' my uncle called me a third time; 'because the palm wine tapper sees what other men do not see, he does not forget he is human and begins to talk to other men as if he is a spirit,' he lashed out at me with his reproving proverb. 'Because what the palm wine tapper taps makes men see and talk to spirits, the palm wine tapper does not think he is a god that makes spirits out of men,' he went on in the same haunting tone. 'Certainly, a man who will not submit to anything will one day submit to the burial mat,' he birched me with his most popular proverb.

For the fourth time, I did not say anything. But what he said to me on this occasion sank deep into me. I did not say anything partly because of how deep what he said struck me. Yet, I never put to use the wise counsel he gave me.

Chapter Eight

I believed in God and believed strongly in heaven. There were three reasons I believed in God. First, I believed in God because I was brought up to believe in him. I started hearing about God from my mother and father before I started hearing about anything else. My mother breastfed me with God the way she breastfed me with her milk. But while she weaned me of her milk, no one weaned me of belief in God. The second reason I believed in God was that without God creating man, man would just be an animal without meaning and hope of future existence. The third reason I believed in God was that there was nothing else to believe in.

As I grew and began seeing the harsh realities of life, my faith in God was severely tested but vanity in me would not let me give up my faith in a Supreme Being. I encountered situations in life that did not make sense if there was God, yet I continued to believe in God. I saw abjectly poor people who were very hard-working, but could barely feed. I saw imbeciles who could not think and mad people sleeping in the open without clothes and food. I saw deaf and dumb people. I saw cripples and blind people. I saw rich people living in mansions. I met very intelligent people whose brains gave them all the best chances in life. All these people were supposed to have been created by the same God who on the last day would judge all of them. This did not make sense to me; yet I continued to believe in God. All these people were not equally taught; why should they equally be examined? But I continued to believe in God. In the close chambers of sense, whatever does not make sense is thrown out of the window. But in my open chambers of faith, it was things that did not make sense that doors and arms were open for.

Apart from encountering situations that did not make sense if there is God, I created some of these situations. I raided and sold people into slavery, yet God did not do anything. I ill-treated my servants, yet God was silent. I was arrogant and haughty, yet God did not bring me down from my high horse. The only occasions I came close to seeing God stepping into human affairs to assert his presence was when my father was sick and I attributed his sickness to divine punishment. But if my father was being punished on earth, why should he be punished again in the hereafter? That would be double punishment.

I believed in God without knowing who God is and believed in heaven without knowing where heaven is and what it looks like. It seemed I was not alone in my lack of knowledge of who God is and where heaven is. All other believers in God were for the most part like me.

I not only believed in God and heaven, I believed that what I was on earth, I will be in heaven. If I am rich on earth, I will be rich in heaven. If I am poor on earth, I will be poor in heaven. Whatever is bound on earth is bound in heaven; and as it is on earth, it is in heaven. Part of my struggle to be rich on earth was to avoid poverty in heaven.

The basis of my faith in God and heaven was a simple one: Man is such an important and critical being on earth that his life cannot just end on earth. It must continue elsewhere. A Supreme Being is the only being that makes this feasible. I saw men being born like animals and dying like animals, yet I believed man is a special being. I saw men struggling for food like animals, going hungry like animals, falling sick like animals, excreting like animals and having sex like animals, yet I believed they were different beings from animals with a special destiny animals do not have.

My belief that man is a special being different from animals was founded on the fact that man wears clothes; animals do not; man lives in houses; animals do not; Man is intelligent; animals are not; man thinks; animals do not; man talks; animals do not. All these things I credited man with and debited animals with I did not look closely at them in crediting one with and debiting the other with.

Man wears clothes. This is not an expression of strength but weakness. If he does not wear clothes, cold and insect bites will kill him. Animals do not need clothes. They are sufficient with their fur. Man lives in houses. This also is not an expression of strength but weakness. If he does not live in a house, he will die. Animals do not need houses. Those of them that need houses live in holes and caves. Man is intelligent. That is the only weapon he has in life. Without it, he wouldn't have survived natural selection just as the skunk wouldn't have without smell or the snake without poison. Animals do not need such intelligence for survival. And who is man to say animals are not intelligent when we see intelligence every day in their survival strategies; when I could see more intelligence in my dog than in my bodyguards. Man thinks. He has to or perishes. And who are we to say animals do not think? Man talks; how do we know animals do not talk when we do not understand their languages. When we don't understand what a dog is saying we say the dog is barking. In so saying, we are debiting our stupidity and crediting the dog with it. In so doing, our weakness becomes the dog's weakness and its strength our strength.

The God we claim created us special beings, animals did not create him; we created him. If animals created a God for themselves, they would be the special beings of their God. If they didn't create a God, they are perhaps far more intelligent and less vain to create one.

Chapter Nine

My life was a Narcissistic one. Governed by vanity, pride and arrogance, I cannot tell the story of my life without repeatedly returning to vanity, pride and arrogance. Neither can I tell it without repeatedly returning to my haughty and deluded bearing on life.

When not attending to my business, I was more likely to be on the street flaunting my wealth than at home or elsewhere in sober reflection. On the street, I expected everyone I met to stop and admire me or at least regard me. Whenever anyone walked past me without seeming to notice me, I was sorely grieved. I was too important not to be noticed or to be ignored. The colours I adorned myself with were too loud not to be seen or heard on the street. How could such a slight fellow walk past me without paying the toll of regard to me? Didn't he know I am Tata the Maghot of the land? Did he even need to know who I was? Merely seeing me on the road should tell him I was someone important that courtesies of regard must be paid to. Surely, I will find a way of dealing with him.

As I expected men to observe respect towards me, I sometimes expected the sun, trees, animals and birds to do the same. When the day is cool and I set out of my house to enjoy the cool day outside, and the sun along the way begins to blaze out heat, I would wonder why the sun should be so hot when it knows I am outside under it. And the air; why was it still instead of blowing to fan me? I sometimes scolded the ground for not springing under my feet when I am walking on it so that it delivers me to the royalty of the sky. I also sometimes rebuked the water in nearby streams and ponds for not rushing to the path I walked to wash my dusty feet. When the weather cools while I was outside, I was exultant. The weather was doing what it should by me.

When the wind rustled the leaves of trees making them whistle and whisper, I thought the wind must be drumming and piping my praise on the leaves. When I heard a bird singing a melodious song nearby, I believed the bird must be singing my praise.

The holy scriptures say all things were created for man. I believed this is the case. But why are the things God created for man not doing the bidding of man I often wondered in anger. I like eating antelope and grass-cutter meat. Why can't I when in need of the meat of these animals call any of them to come to me for me to eat it? Why must I hunt for them the same way the tiger and the lion do? Man is a special being and I am man. Why am I struggling for survival the way animals and birds – ordinary beings, are?

My initial thinking was that man was created last after all other things had been created so that he could have the use of the things that were created before him. God knowing what man would need created all the things he would need before creating him. He would need the sun to work; the sun was created. He would need the night to rest; the night was created. He would need trees for fruits, medicine and shade; they were created. He would need animals for meat and perhaps labour; they were created. Why then were these things not doing the bidding of man? Why must man struggle for them the same way other beings they were not created for have to struggle for them?

The cock is crowing to wake me up I sometimes thought. But is the cock crowing to wake me up or because this is the time it usually crows? Rain is falling so that I can cultivate my farm and plant my crops. But is rain falling because of me or because conditions for rain to fall have arisen in the atmosphere? When I thought this way, I felt my head was all screwed up on the wrong side of my neck. The cock is crowing to wake me up; rain is falling for me to farm and plant my crops. I am the only reason things happen. Without me the cock will not crow and rain would not fall.

If God will take the pain of creating all things for the wellbeing of man, it means man must be very important to God. For man to be very important to the Supreme Being, it means he must be very useful to him. What is the use of man to God? I could not see any beyond the claim that man is meant to serve and worship God. Is God so vain to take all the pains of creating all things and man just to be served and worshipped? Whenever I thought this way, I knew I was thinking in a blasphemous way and must stop thinking that way.

If all things were created for man, will all things cease to be if man ceased to be? I often found my mind returning to this question. Will all trees die because man is dead? Will the water in the rivers, streams and the seas dry up because man is dead? All these seemed to me unlikely. Later yet I started wondering if the creation of man was an afterthought; I started wondering if man was created at all; if anything was created at all; if things just evolved because conditions for their evolution were in existence. I even wondered if there is any being called God. This was blasphemy in its worse, pure and undiluted form and I had to stop thinking this way.

There is God who created all things and created human beings as special beings to enjoy all the things he created. Man is a special creation of God worthy of his energetic and spiritual attention. Man can't be anything other than a special being. The occasional pathetic condition of man may sometimes suggest otherwise, but the greatness of man affirms he is a special being. The greatness of man? Yes, the greatness of man I shook my head against a contrary thought in my mind.

I thought a lot about heaven and hell. Heaven; where is it? Well, I don't know where it is and it seemed no one knows. But somehow there is such a place. Things won't make sense without it. Hell; where is it? Well, I don't know where it is and it seemed no one knows. But somehow there is such a place. Things won't make sense without it. These places must exist for man to be a special being worthy of life in a hereafter.

Chapter Ten

As children, we hunted a lot in the bushes around our small town and in the forest. By my financial circumstances, I needed not to hunt because I had all the meat I needed at home. But out of an adventurous spirit, I always followed my age mates to hunt against the counsel of my father.

We hunted mostly for rabbits, bandicoot rats, and where we found them, antelopes. Most of our hunting was in the dry season. To hunt, we usually set the bush or forest ablaze. In the dry season, the forest and the bush were good fuel for fire, and fire always hungry and thirsty, gulped it down its throat in quantum quaffs. The fire we lighted the bush or forest with would race through the forest burning grasses and scorching trees we did not intend to scorch; trees we often felt bad had been burned. The footprints we always left behind as hunters were always a charred forest or bush we often felt unpleasant going into afterwards.

In the beginning, when we set a bush ablaze, we used to kill many animals that were the target of our hunting. These were mostly bandicoot rats, bush rats and rabbits. As the fire would be burning, these animals would run out of their hiding places in the forest or bush and we will set after them with sticks and arrows. As the animals will be running for safety, birds on trees would be flying about in the sky with nowhere to perch. In the sky with the birds would be palls of smoke that would then be the clouds over our sky. Sometimes the smoke was so bad that it made people cough and drew tears from eyes.

As time went by, we found ourselves burning forests and bushes for little or no animal kill. Sometimes after burning an entire bush or forest, we had little games to show for the bush or forest we had burned. It was either that the animals had fled our forests and bushes because of loss of habitat or fear of being hunted by fire or they had gone extinct. Burning of forests and bushes led to animal extinction through loss of habitat and killing of the animals by our clubs, bows and arrows. Animals lucky to escape death from hunting and loss of habitat were most likely to flee to safer regions.

When a bush or forest was set on fire in the beginning of the dry season when crops were yet to be harvested from farms, the fires sometime strayed into farms burning crops. At all times, fruit trees like mango and cashew trees were always burned by these fires. Though burning the bush and forest caused much havoc to the forest, bush and farmlands, I could not remember any serious effort by elders of our town or authority to stop bush and forest burning.

Later in life, I liken what we did to the forest and the bush in the name of hunting to what I heard ancients of Gursa did to trees they wanted their fruits: They cut down the trees to harvest the fruits. One day while hunting for bandicoot rats and other animals after burning a big track of forest land with only a bandicoot rat killed, I began lamenting our action to Gyendo who I was hunting with.

'Bush and forest burning to hunt for animals no longer makes sense to me,' I said. 'Look at the forest we have burned, and look at what we have as the gain of our labour.'

'Actually, the game does not seem to be worth the candle,' Gyendo said. But at least we have gotten something. But for the fire, we wouldn't have caught this bandicoot rat.'

'You are right we probably wouldn't have caught the bandicoot rat without the fire; but we certainly wouldn't have burned the forest,' I said.

'We don't eat the forest; but we eat the bandicoot rat,' Gyendo said.

'You are always thinking of food,' I said.

'You are not always thinking of food because you have a lot of it,' Gyendo said. 'You hunt as a hobby; I hunt to live.'

I did not say anything.

'What is there to think about in life outside food?' Gyendo said after a while of silence.

'We may not be eating the forest we enjoy its shade,' I said at last.

'You can only enjoy a shade with a full stomach.'

'With a full stomach without fresh air to breathe, you may suffocate.'

'Hunger will suffocate you before foul air does.'

'What we do to the forest in the name of hunting is what we do to the river in the name of fishing,' I went on as if I had not heard what Gyendo said. 'To catch fish, we poison the whole river with toxic substances. I don't see any wisdom in this. Why kill a river to eat fish?

Sometimes it is not only the river we kill, we kill ourselves; the fish we killed through poison, we eat the fish with poison inside it and began our slow, if not quick death.'

'If we go by your fears, we will not eat,' Gyendo said. 'We use manure to grow our crops. The crops take up the manure and we eat them with the manure they have absorbed.'

'You are saying something there.'

'We are in a trap. We have to go along with life on the terms it is presenting to us whether the terms are for life or death.'

The soot generated by our bushfires I was told was nothing compared to the smog generated by locomotive trains in England. I was told that as a train rattled on the rail-track through forests and towns, it emitted palls of smoke that shot into the sky in dark balls before spreading out into the atmosphere. Leaves of trees by the rail track were all loaded with the soot the way a river is loaded with sand. I wondered what would become of the forest in that country if this goes on forever. I wondered if the comfort of travelling by rail was worth the soot the train was loading on the atmosphere. I wondered if travelling by horse or donkey was not better than this. I even wondered if trekking was not better. But I was soon myself once more: A man after the fanciful and beautiful things of life. The train despite the soot it emitted was a fanciful and colourful thing that excited me to no end. I prayed and longed for the day the train would come to my own country.

Chapter Eleven

I had a dog I was so fond of and was so fond of me. I had an intimacy with Lolo my dog that I did not have with any human being. I also had trust in him that I had in no human being.

If I was open to learning, I would have learned humility and obedience from Lolo. Whatever I wanted Lolo to do, he did. If I wanted him to follow me somewhere, he did. If I wanted him to stay at home, he did. Often, he did what I desired of him without me asking. He seemed to read my mind so perfectly well. There were so many ways my dog could be said to be more humane than me and I more bestial than him. He knew when to bark and when not to; knew when to walk with his tail up in the air and when not to; knew when to follow me about and when not to. Unlike my dog, I did not know when to talk and when not to; when to be arrogant, if there was ever such time, and when not to. Unlike my dog that was loyal to me, I was loyal to no one but myself. Unlike my dog that always considered my interest, I considered no one's interest. Only my interest mattered. Unlike my dog that made sacrifices for me, I made no sacrifice for no one but expected people to make sacrifices for me.

Whenever I sat to contemplate my life, it seemed the only genuine being in it was Lolo and Lolo was a dog. Even I was not a genuine being in my own life. I was not true to anyone and no one was true to me. Even Lolo was true to me not so much because of my being true to him, but because he was a creature of truth.

Whenever I looked at my dog, I marveled at it; I wondered what was going on in its mind, for I believed it had a mind. Only a creature with a mind would behave the way my dog was behaving. What was it thinking of me and of itself? What was it thinking of the world and what was going on in the world? Sometimes looking at it I was moved to emotion to hug it and cuddle it to myself. On one of such emotional moments while I was hugging it, I spoke to it.

'You are such a wonderful dog. Are there other dogs like you in the country; in the world? Which clan and tribe do you come from? What do you think of me? What do you think of the world? Where do you get your good manners from? From which well of patience do you draw your patience from? What are you seeing that I am not seeing?

When I spoke to my dog, I believed it understood me. I also believed it spoke to me whenever it released a humming bark. It was just that I did not understand it.

One evening I went out for a walk as I usually did and my dog followed me as it sometimes did. Along the way we met an old woman and a little girl walking in the direction we were coming from. Unlike me taking a walk, the old woman and the little girl looked like they were on a journey and had trekked a great deal. The little girl walking behind the old woman was carrying something wrapped in a piece of white cloth toned brown by age and use. The two travelers not only looked tired and hungry, they looked frightened by something.

The path we walked on was a narrow one that required one of two people walking on it in opposite directions to step aside for the other when they meet on the path. By age and the frailty of the woman, I supposed to be the one to step aside, but I did not. I walked into her making her stagger perilously into the bush.

I walked on without looking back or showing remorse. I walked on pursued by the reproving and haunting sayings of my uncle: *Because the palm wine tapper sees what other men do not see, he does not forget he is human and begins to talk to other men as if he is a spirit; because what the palm wine tapper taps makes men see and talk to spirits, the palm wine tapper does not think he is a god that makes spirits out of men; a man who will not submit to anything will one day submit to the burial mat.* When I eventually looked back the old woman was stooping over her walking stick by the path staring at my retreating form. The little girl was by her crying. My dog was nowhere to be seen. It had gone back home. I was not surprised my dog was not behind me. Any time I put up this kind of behaviour, my dog would leave me apparently in protest.

For a while, I was gripped by remorse and shame, but soon shrugged the twosome off. Lolo had his life to live and I had mine. If he wanted to be so conscientious and nice in an unconscionable and nasty world, that was his headache. I had my own headache and could not bear his own in addition to mine.

Because Lolo was not following me, I turned to head back home where I was sure I would find him. I walked past the old woman still standing by the wayside shaken by what I had done to her. When I walked past her, she shook her head at me in astonishment and grief. I walked on without a care if the world was aghast and stunned by my action.

Lolo like Dimma ought to have been a mirror I would view myself, but alas he was not. I carried on with Lolo the same arrogant and self-conceited way I had always carried on without hearing the intelligence my dog was always barking to me. Instead of Lolo being the dog that could no longer hear the whistle of its owner, I was the owner that could not hear the whistle of his dog. The tail was wagging the dog instead of the dog wagging the tail and all was right with me. Somehow Lolo endured me because of who he was, despite who I was.

Chapter Twelve

A couple of months ago, Ajo one of the young men I captured and sold into slavery was a more virile youth than any I had ever sold. Usually I did not know the names of the slaves I sold. But Ajo was so exceptional that I knew his name. Broad featured and tall, he was a very imposing fellow if also a terror-inspiring fellow. When he walked, he bounced as if he had springs under his feet that kept throwing him up to the roll of the sky. By mere sight, he was a man with brute strength, and I suspected one with a mean heart. When I captured him, he stayed in my slave camp for only a day before I took him to the coast to sell him to the white men. The night he spent in my camp, I did not sleep much that night. Though he was chained, I was afraid he would use his brute strength to break the barricade; free himself and other slaves and assault me. Because of his health and physique, I sold him at a very high price. Later, I thought the slave merchant who bought him at such a ransom price did not think well. Possessing such ferocious strength, he would be source of fear of breaking free and doing violence to his owner as he would be a source of great labour. My thinking turned out right, not only to the loss of the white man who bought him but my danger who sold him. Shortly after the ship he was set sail, he had somehow unlocked his chains and jumped into the sea. Being a good swimmer, he easily swam to shore and began his search for me to exert vengeance.

I was in my house one evening when I sighted Ajo from afar. Though I was with him for less than two days, I could tell his form in the night. The moment I saw him, I knew he must have broken away from the white man I sold him to and was coming for me for vengeance. It seemed Lolo also recognized him and like me knew why he was in our neighbourhood, for he started barking at him while he was not yet near the house.

For a while, I stood looking at Ajo drawing near my house in his bouncing walk that took him into the air and brought him back to earth. As he drew nearer the house, he was bouncing less. As he drew nearer more, his walk turned to that of a stalker. I stood looking at him in a hazy kind of vision too numbed by fear to do anything. I could not think; I could not act; I could even scarcely breathe. A thick fog had developed in my head and chest that had frozen thinking and action, and was freezing breathing also. The rapidity of Lolo's barking also was not helping matters. He was letting out long-string siren kind of barking I had come to associate with approaching danger.

Two arsenals were necessary for the business of slave trade: Guns and bodyguards. I had a gun and had bodyguards. The gun I inherited from my father who was the first person to own a gun in our town; the bodyguards I recruited myself. When Ajo arrived my neighbourhood, the gun was in the house but none of my bodyguards was around. Often, I was sick of their prowling presence and wanted to be left alone to talk to myself or to a friend or relation that had visited. When I was sick of their presence, I told them to go home and returned later. Now none of them was around and Ajo was about in all his sinister and fearsome presence.

Soon Lolo burst into my room barking and wagging his tail about like a whisk. This was his way of telling me danger was about and I should be about my defence. This action of Lolo thawed my paralysis and I sprang into action. Moving fast but quietly like a shadow, I left the room I was and went into the room I was keeping my gun. It was an old Dane gun that had seen years and action than the tortoise had seen swamps and tricks.

My gun was always loaded with gun-powder and that was why I kept it where I may not touch it off accidentally. I carried the gun from the corner of the room and again walked quietly out of the room the way I walked into it. In a moment I was back to the room I was earlier – the room I saw Ajo approaching my house like a charging bull out for a kill. I peeped outside, but did not see him. But I was as sure as death he was lurking somewhere about the house working and waiting for an opportunity to strike. For a while, I was in two minds. One mind told me to fire into the air to tell Ajo what he was up against; another mind told me to keep my arsenals under cover for a surprise which is the strongest weapon one could have against a malevolent presence like Ajo. In the end, I decided to uncover my arsenals by firing into the air. Let Ajo know who and what he was up against.

After firing into the air, I listened for the sound of some kind of movement from Ajo but heard none. I was not unduly surprised. Ajo impressed me as a hard-boiled character good at the game we were playing. I continued to wait and listened for the sound of his movement, but none came. Though I did not hear any sound or saw any movement from him, I knew he was still around the house. Nothing told me this like the continuous barking of Lolo. Whenever he barked like this, danger was about.

I was still waiting and listening when I saw my bodyguards coming towards the house. When I saw their approach, I was elated. I was no longer alone. Two other people were joining me. So Ajo was now up against three men. The only snag was that my bodyguards did not know a menacing presence like Ajo was lurking around and so may fall easy prey to him. However, if they were a little bit more intelligent, they would have had a sense of danger from the way Lolo was barking. But they were stupid men Lolo was far more intelligent than.

With knowledge of Ajo's presence, every step my bodyguards took as they walked towards the house was a fearful one for me and would have been a more fearful one for the bodyguards if they were seised of my knowledge. All of a sudden, a gun cracked into life tossing my two bodyguards into the air. I was shocked by the weirdness of it all. I almost ran out of the house towards the fallen bodyguards, but quickly realizing the danger of doing so, forbore.

For some time thereafter, Lolo continued to bark, then stopped. When he stopped, he walked back into the room I was. When Lolo stopped barking and came into my room, I knew danger had abated; I knew Ajo was no longer around the house. With Lolo in tow, I walked to the two fallen bodyguards and found them spurting blood where bullets had ripped open their chests. They were both dead.

Chapter Thirteen

For days, I was gripped by a morbid fear over the way Ajo killed my two bodyguards and the professional way he left my house without me knowing when and how he left. When I saw him bouncing towards the house, I did not see him carrying any gun. But apparently, he carried one most likely strapped behind him. Where did he find such a sophisticated gun? Most likely from the white man he escaped from.

The clinical way Ajo killed my bodyguards and the way he left my house told me he was a thoroughbred professional who could have killed me and my dog if he had wanted to, despite the fact that I had a gun. As a professional, he knew the type of gun I had from the sound it made when I fired it into the air and also knew its limitations and would have exploited these limitations. Why then did he not kill me and my dog? I was perplexed by the inexplicable.

When my fear began to abate and I could think better, my mind went back to how my slave catchers caught Ajo. He was caught in a dragnet while relieving his bowels in a bush. My slave catchers had sneaked up to him with dragnet and had thrown it over him so abruptly he had no chance escaping. Armed with chains, they had chained both his legs and hands and delivered him to me who sold him to the white man. I was by the seaside when the ship he was set sail to Europe. For him to break ship and swam out of the sea showed he was an immensely capable man. If I had any doubt of his capabilities, what he did to my guardsmen removed that doubt. I had no doubt he could have killed me after killing my bodyguards or even before killing them if that was what he wanted. The motive was there and the opportunity was also there; why then did he not kill me? Did he want to terrorise me before killing me? Was this what he wanted? It seemed to me to be what he wanted. If it was what he wanted, then I was up for a long-drawn terror.

After his first wave of attack, I did not see or hear of Ajo again until when I was almost forgetting his threat to my life. One night I was sleeping in my room when a faint, then a loud tap on my window woke me up. I sat up in bed in fear and confusion. Even in my fear and confusion I immediately knew the presence by my window outside was Ajo. Who else could it be if not him?

How did he know the window I was sleeping by? Where was Lolo? Why was he not barking? His barking supposed to have waked me from sleep on him sensing the approach of Ajo. Had Ajo killed him? I was alarmed by this thought and started sweating profusely. Lolo was the only chance I had against Ajo; if he was gone, my chances were all gone with him. Then I heard Lolo's barking outside. Why was it that it was now I was hearing his barking? From what I knew of Lolo, he must have been barking on Ajo's approach to the house. Why then did his barking not wake me up from sleep? Am I now so used to his barking the way I was used to the chirr sounds of crickets or the croaking of a frog as to sleep through it? When I woke up from Ajo's loud tap on my window, why did I not hear Lolo's barking? In the fear and confusion I was, could I have heard his barking? I doubted it. Where were my guardsmen and bodyguards? Were they asleep? Why was I paying them ransoms as salaries? Were they complicit in the terror Ajo was holding before me? Being arrogant and spiteful, I was the type of person that can easily make his subordinates betray him.

Lolo only barked when danger was approaching me. But when danger attacked me, he went beyond barking to attacking whoever was attacking me. When I sat to consider his attitude, I could see the wisdom in it. By only barking when danger was merely approaching, he was making things safer for both him and me. If he was attacking every danger that was approaching me, both he and I would have had a lot to repent of.

Returning to Ajo by my window, he was still tapping the window intermittently – doing the devil's tattoo. Ping-pong the tapping went on in the most disconcerting manner. Whoever was doing the devil's tattoo was surely the devil out to wear me out and he was very much succeeding in what he was about. I was being reduced to a bundle of nerves.

Though I was convinced the presence outside was Ajo, I still had doubt it was him, since I had not actually seen him. If he was not the one who was it? This thought alarmed and frightened me more than the thought of Ajo being the one by the window. Bad as Ajo's threat was, I was subconsciously, if not consciously, getting used to it. The possibility of another threat from a different source scared me to my marrow.

After tapping the window for a long time, the tapping stopped and never returned again that night, but returned several other nights in different forms and shapes. Shortly after the tapping stopped, Lolo's barking also stopped. This told me Ajo was gone, if indeed it was him that was tapping the window.

Chapter Fourteen

I married my wife quite late in life. For a long time, I strutted and flaunted myself on the street forgetting to marry. When I remembered to do so, I found myself a very beautiful maiden.

My wife was a very beautiful woman I was twenty years older than. Youthful and beautiful, I believed she married me for my wealth and not any love she had for me. Anyone looking at us could see it was not love that was between us, but money and lust. She only wanted my money and I only wanted her body.

When I was courting her, I was all love; she was my heartbeat and my heartthrob. The moment I married her however, my love for her seemed to have flown out of all the doors and windows of my life. My heartbeat turned to my heartache. Things got so bad that I sometimes wondered if I ever courted her. When I remembered some of the sweet things I used to say to her while courting her, I felt sick for they now sounded stupid to me.

The affair between my wife and I was as stormy as it was deceitful and fake. Hardly a day passed without us quarrelling or having some misunderstanding. There was no love to conceal faults. So, she saw all my faults and I saw all her faults. Rashes on my body were boils to her and dust on her feet was mud to me. What I did not like my wife seemed to like and what she did not like, I seemed to like.

I don't mind noise. My wife resented noise as if it were a plague. Any time there was noise, it seemed to disturb her beauty and this sometimes used to make me happy. Her beauty should now and then be disturbed. All through day and night she was silent as if she was forbidden to speak. All through day and night, she sat quietly by herself while her beauty flowed loudly around her so much that I suspected she was quiet so that her beauty could be heard.

Whatever my wife lacked in speech however, she made up in hearing. Her hearing sense was so sharp that she could hear a dry leaf falling outside. If her mouth was always idle, her ears were always working overtime. Because she heard faint as loud noise, she heard any movement about the house and it tended to irritate her if out of tune with the serenity she craved for.

Late in my life, I wondered if I missed out on wisdom talking. I wondered if wisdom used to visit me but every time it came, it will find me talking and would walk away. Why was I always talking anyway? Who do I want to hear me and for what consequence? Wouldn't I be of more moment if I keep my peace? What do I even talk about anyway? When I thought like this, I came close to be less garrulous; but only close.

Because I liked talking a lot, noise was something we did not frequently lack in our house. I was always talking with a friend, a relation that had visited or talking alone to myself. Most of my talking was about myself and what I had achieved in life; how the world was lucky to have a fellow like me. When talking got loud, my wife was often driven to such distraction as to be a neurotic wreck.

'All the yawping; all the racket you generate around this house, doesn't it ever worry you that it distresses your wife?' she asked me one day when I had finished talking with a relation who had left.

'Yawping!'

'Yes, yawping.'

'So, my talks are yawps.'

'Before you imagined they were orations?'

'Why should it distress me?' I asked in a rasping voice that seemed to rattle the room we were as it rattled her. 'If your silence does not disturb me, why should my noise disturb you?'

I don't like heat. My wife did not seem to mind it. I was always opening the windows of our house in cold as in hot seasons and she was always closing them. In all weather she bathed with hot water. What was she cooking or baking with all the heat about her, I could not say. Her beauty was already cooked and baked and it was what she was serving me; so, what was she cooking or baking again?

'Don't close that window!' I shouted at her one day when she was closing a window I had opened.

'So that all the noise in this lousy town will come in?' she asked cynically.

'No; so that some fresh air can flow in and take away some stench I am perceiving in something in the house,' I said in a petulant tone.

'Tata, marrying you is my only mistake in life. Your faults are too distressing for happiness,' she said sullenly.

'There are two mistakes here my dear; yours and mine,' I said in a grating tone.

Ours was a marriage both spouses were on edge and easily tipped over into a quarrel or fight. If there are marriages made in heaven, there are those made in hell. Ours was one of the marriages made in hell and was therefore hellish. When Ajo, if indeed it was Ajo who was haunting me, started turning up in my house at night, I was without wife. My wife had since left. Having no children, I was alone in my house with only Lolo and my bodyguards who I still did not know why I was retaining them.

Chapter Fifteen

Dejana and I were age mates. We grew up together in the same small town and attended the local school together. However, while my father was rich, Dejana's father was poor. I could afford good clothes and shoes, Dejana could not. In my imperial arrogance, I always looked at Dejana in a condescending, contemptuous manner whenever our paths crossed. One day, not contented with mere facial expression, I gave verbal expression to my feelings about Dejana's condition. 'Dejana why is your father so poor and you so poor like him? Do you know your poverty is embarrassing this town? Poverty is a disease and whoever is poor is a disease that should be avoided the way the leper is. Yes, poverty is leprosy.'

What I said stabbed Dejana's heart the way a knife might not have. My verbal assault was perhaps worse than any physical assault I could have meted on him. The pain in his heart was so severe that it contorted his face into a hideous tablet. The pain he felt was so much that he could not say anything to me that moment until later. Later, he came to my house and spoke thus to me: 'Tata, you whose father is rich not by any decent or honest labour, but by catching and selling people into slavery has the nerves to insult my father who lives on a decent income? You dare insult my father when your father and yourself are thieves and vampires living on the blood of others?'

'Why can't your own father become a thief and a vampire to free you from the poverty your family is another name of?' I said hurt more by what he said about my father than what he said about me. It was then I realized it was more hurting when one's parents or tribe was insulted than when one was insulted. For a while, I wondered why this was the case without knowing for the moment, but later knowing. Insult of one's parents or tribe goes to one's roots; it is insult of one's origin and essence and this is far worse than insult of one's person which most often goes only to one's behaviour or quality, not to his essence.

'Tata, I assure you, you will pay for the insult you heaped on my family today,' Dejana swore with passion. 'You will pay and pay until you can't pay anymore; until you are bankrupt from paying; until you die from paying. It will not be today you will pay, but I assure you some day you will pay.' Saying this, he left my house with the anger he came with. Such was his anger that he seemed to have left with more anger than he came with.

Since that day, any time I met Dejana I could see in his eyes the hurt I inflicted on him and the hate he had for me. But neither his hurt nor hate bothered me much. In a fleeting moment I may be bothered by the hate but not the hurt. Indeed, I tended to enjoy the hurt.

Though I kept seeing hate in Dejana's eyes, I gave little credence to his threat of making me pay for my insult of him and his family. I saw his threat as one of the empty threats one keeps receiving in his interaction with life. It was only when Ajo appeared and started haunting me that I began thinking of Dejana who I had also wronged in the past. Dejana said I will pay and pay without telling me how I will pay. Well, Dejana was dead. He died before he could make me pay.

I was a deeply superstitious person. Was the spirit of Dejana up against me doing what Dejana could not do in his life time? Was his spirit by my window? He had said I will pay and pay until I can't pay anymore; until I am bankrupt from paying; until I die paying. Was this his way of making me pay? If it was, he was surely making me bankrupt from paying. I had to be engaging guardsmen and bodyguards who I was paying ransoms as salaries. I was dying of fright; he was surely killing me from paying.

But Dejana was not the only one I had trampled on in my pride and arrogance; so why was I thinking only of him? Was it because I knew him more intimately or because he threatened me with reprisal more brazenly? Some people I had stepped on might not have said anything, but may do worse things to me than those who threatened me. Who was by my window among the scores of people I had hurt that were coming out for me?

There was the old poor woman I recently walked into on the path. Was she human or spirit? Was she the person that was appearing to me as Ajo? No doubt Ajo was a very strong person, but with all his strength, how could he have escaped from a ship he was boarded in chains and swam out of the sea to hunt and haunt me? No, it was not Ajo that was haunting me. It must be the old woman or Dejana's spirit. The fact that my guardsmen and bodyguards had not been able to secure me against this nocturnal harassment further strengthened my belief that I was up against something much more sinister than Ajo.

My room for a long time was a fortress for me against the vindictive spirits I thought were up in arms against me. It remains a fortress for a long time until one night I heard someone moving in my room without seeing him. I froze in fear. Later I heard someone laughing very close to me. I could no longer remain in the room. I fled into the night pursued by the laughing presence.

Chapter Sixteen

I kept running and the presence, if spirit, the spirit pursuing me kept laughing until I could run no more. I fell on my knees and then on my belly with my hands in my ears trying to cut off the laughter. But the laugher was now in my head. So, I could not cut it off.

While I ran, I had a feeling the ground I was running on was also running. Now on the ground, I had a feeling the ground was opening up to swallow me. When it was almost swallowing me, it would vomit me out again.

For a long time, I writhed on the ground in paranoia. I was surprised Lolo did not attack my pursuer or even bark at him. It was much later it occurred to me my dog might not have heard the laughter of my pursuer. It was later it occurred to me I was the only one tormented by his laughter. May be my pursuer who was likely to be my victim wanted only me to suffer for my misdeeds. Maybe he was not laughing outside me but inside my head. But if Lolo was not hearing his laughter, was he also not hearing my screams? Was I screaming into my intestines? Was Lolo dead? Then I heard Lolo barking and whirling round. Why was he only barking and whirling round? Why had he not bit the person assaulting me? But how could he bite a spirit, for I was now convinced it was a spirit that was terrorizing me. No human being could do this to me and I was unable to get a glimpse of him all the while of my flight from my house to where I was writing on the ground. While running I had looked back but saw no one; yet someone was close on my heels laughing into my ears.

For quite a while, I kept wailing and writhing on the ground until I passed out. I did not come to until the wee hours of the morning. When I came to, it was very cold where I was and I suspected it was the cold that snapped me out of my blackout. Everywhere was quiet. There was no more laughter and my dog was no longer barking. But it was there by my side as it had always been whenever I was in danger. That it was not barking told me as usual that danger had withered.

After lying on the ground a while more, I stood up and looked around me. Now the night was much less dark than before. The clouded sky had shed its clouds and the stars in the sky were now beaming their light on the earth. The sky which before was under a blanket was now bare with all the eyes in it blinking as they stared at me. About me, menacing figures in rank and file were looming out of the ground also staring at me. Shrubs and trees I used to pat in the day time were now monsters out to devour me. My fears were back. I started fleeing back home. As I ran home, the dark figures of the night seemed to creep forward on me. Behind me my dog was also running; but it was not barking. This again told me no one was after me. I calmed down and stopped running but continued walking home. I could think now. This is all very unfair. What have I done to anyone to merit this haunting? I have heard of witch-hunting several times, but had never given it serious thought; had never thought of it in a literal sense. Is this what those hunted by witches go through? Just as I was getting my thoughts into order again, the laughter broke out again. It sounded like people snapping dry faggots in my ears. I was once more running. Behind me my dog was also running; and this time it was barking. Its barking turned my fright to paranoia.

Both I and my dog ran on pursued by dementing laughter that rang out of the sky like the songs of the bell of Guudu* and vibrated in the caves of the night like echoes of doom. I kept running pursued by the laughter until we were by our house. Then the laughter once more ceased. I was all broken down now as I wobbled and stumbled into my house. Finding myself on a bed, I fell asleep with my uncle's popular proverb taunting me: *A man who will not submit to anything will one day submit to the burial mat.*

When I woke up, day had since broken. Lying on the bed, I was seized by nostalgia and my mind drifted to the days my father was selling slaves to white men for mirrors, rum and tobacco. I could see how he used to smile into the mirrors with pride and how his throat used to race up and down as he gulped the drink. I could also see the look of satisfaction on his face when he finished taking the drink. How I wish I could have the old strong rum of those days to make me face life with more courage. Rum these days was water by another name. Thinking this way, I began smiling into a mirror by my bedside the way my father used to. This turned out to be the last time I would ever smile into a mirror. This

---

* In Sonke myths, the bell of Guudu tolled songs without being rung by anyone.

turned out to be the last time I would have feelings close to happiness, for my remaining life was overtaken by terror.

Chapter Seventeen

For months, I kept having intermittent nocturnal terror visits in my house by whoever was haunting me. Whoever was haunting me, if human, was too smart for my guardsmen and even my dog as they were never able to confront him. He seemed to always carry a spell with him that he always cast on them sending them to sleep whenever he was around. They only woke up when he was gone. Several times, I changed my guardsmen thinking they were inefficient, but none of the new guardsmen I hired was able to deal with the terror that kept visiting my house. After changing the guardsmen several times without any change in my situation, I stopped and resigned myself to terror. At some point, I thought of fleeing my town to another, but on a second thought decided not to. If I was being haunted by a spirit as it appeared to me, fleeing to another town will not secure me from the nocturnal terror I was afflicted by. I again resigned myself to terror.

About a year after Ajo first visited my house, a terror attack no one ever expected could be carried out on our town overtook the town leaving scores of people dead and scores of others maimed. I and my uncle were lucky to flee the town unscathed to the hiding place I am telling this story from. The terrorists numbering fifteen men armed with guns, bows and arrows invaded our quiet, sleeping town towards sunset when people were retiring to their homes for the night.

The men who later said they were ex-slaves that had fled slavery stormed our town through the forest on the eastern border of the town. They wasted no time in telling everyone who they were: They were ex-slaves who had freed themselves from slavery and were in the town to make it pay for its role in the slave trade. They said they came to attack the village which according to them had acquired notoriety for trading in slaves. The irony however was that those who traded in slaves in the town could be counted on the fingers of one hand.

In making the town pay, everyone in it was a fair game and legitimate target. They said all they had eaten in their lives was hatred and were in the town to vomit what they had eaten. They said once upon a time, they were served hatred by our town and were in the town to vomit the hatred they were served. The poison they were served could not kill them, but were sure it would kill those they would vomit it on. If there was love in the world, the terrorists said they had not seen or known it and therefore had none to give. The only thing they had seen and known all their lives was hatred which they were pregnant with and were in the town to deliver.

When they came to the town, the armed men all looked like they had had a long trek and were very tired. But as soon as they started shooting people, the fatigue in them seemed to have shed off and they had acquired new energy and vigour as they sprayed the village with bullets and arrows. People ran helter-skelter and as they ran, they were mowed down by bullets and arrows. Shrieks and screams of terror spread through the town like the cry of Hondu.[*] Violence and death were about and men and beasts were in flight in wild terror. When the shooting stopped, over ninety people had been shot dead and about twice this number was wounded. Sorrow hung over the town like a stranded dark cloud.

____

[*] In Tekwa mythology, Hondu was a giant who could wake up the whole land in one long strident cry.

For most of that night, lamentation rent the air in Touka. Violence and death had visited the town in a most horrid and contemptuous manner no one could have ever imagined. Touka was not the only slave trading post in the country. There were several other trading posts that were even more notorious for slave trade than Touka. None of such towns had ever been attacked in this ferocious manner; why should the town be selected for this kind of horrendous attack.

'Before something bad happens to you, seldom do you ever contemplate such bad thing can happen to you,' my uncle said. 'Before this attack, I never thought there is so much bitterness and hatred in the world that can be vomited with such ferocity.'

'What happened is indeed shocking even to me who has been in the violent trade of slave trade for decades,' I said.

'I find the attack difficult to understand and explain,' my uncle said. 'How can fellow human beings deal so cruelly with their kind?'

'I really wonder,' I said my mind half with my uncle and half with memories of some of the cruel things I had done to slaves as a slave merchant.

'I think the world is sick,' my uncle said. 'It is only in a sick world something like this can happen. What sense does it make killing someone that has never wronged you?' he seemed to be wondering to himself. 'Almost all the people killed in this attack were not slave merchants. If the terrorists are ex-slaves as they claim, what sense does it make for them killing people that did not enslave them?'

'Hmm ...,' I hummed.

'While being well, you can't be happy in a sick world. The only way you can be happy in such a world is to be sick like everyone,' my uncle said. 'Slaughtering people without any trace of pity? Ah ...'

'It is so damning.'

'You can now see why I had always wanted you to stop being a slave merchant?' my uncle said after a while of silence. 'This nefarious trade like anything evil and unjust can only invite this type of attack. Like begets like.'

'Men who want to be bad will always be bad whether there is slave trade or not,' I said. 'Is it now that slave trade started? Why has there never been this kind of attack? How are we even sure those that attacked us were ex-slaves smarting under a sense of injustice and hitting back at their perceived oppressors. They could just be bad people violating people that had done them no wrong.'

'It is sad.'

'It is indeed sad.'

'It is stupid.'

'It is indeed stupid. If I am stupid in my behaviour, at least I am not the only person who is stupid,' I said after a moment of silence.

'You are indeed not the only one, my son,' my uncle said with a deep sigh. 'All I see happening round the world today is against intelligence. All I see are stupid things that make me sick.'

For a while no one spoke. We were both caught up in our individual thoughts.

'Once again the world has gone mad,' my uncle said, breaking the silence.

'And there does not seem to be anywhere it can be taken for cure,' I intoned

'Even the medicine man has gone mad.'

'And now walks about without his medicine bag laughing at everyone.'

Sitting where we were, I saw Ajo bouncing towards us. I ran out of the cave pursued by Ajo's metallic laughter. My nightmares were back.